TIKTA'LIKTAK

JAMES HOUSTON
TIKTA'LIKTAK
AN INUIT-ESKIMO LEGEND

Harcourt Brace Jovanovich, Publishers

San Diego   New York   London

by the same author

THE WHITE ARCHER: AN INUIT-ESKIMO LEGEND
AKAVAK: AN INUIT-ESKIMO LEGEND

Requests for permission to make copies of any part of the work
should be mailed to: Permissions Department,
Harcourt Brace Jovanovich, Publishers,
Orlando, Florida 32887.

Library of Congress Cataloging-in-Publication Data
Houston, James A., 1921–
Tikta'liktak: an Inuit-Eskimo legend/written and
illustrated by James Houston.
p.   cm.
Summary: A young Eskimo hunter fights for survival while
stranded on an isolated and desolate island.
ISBN 0-15-287748-7 (pbk.)
1. Eskimos — Legends. [1. Eskimos — Legends.
2. Indians of North America — Legends.] I. Title.
E99.E7H86   1990
398.2'089971 — dc20   89-32473

Printed in the United States of America

A B C D E

To John and Sam Houston

and

to Oshaweetok and Ikhaluk

TIKTA'LIKTAK

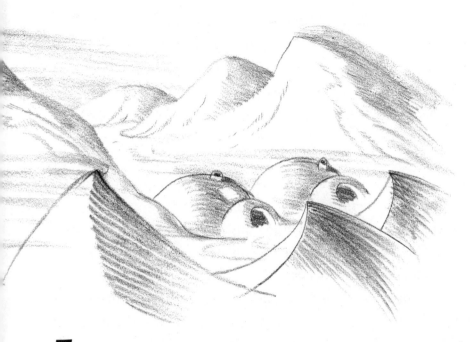

TIKTALIKTAK drove his long sharp chisel into a crack and pulled himself up to the top of the jagged ice. From this height, he looked east and west along the rough barrier ice forced against the coastline as far as he could see.

He looked back along his trail of footprints across the snow-covered shore to his father's igloo, now almost hidden by the three hills that protected it from the howling winds that rushed over their island.

Tiktaliktak's people were sea hunters, singers, carvers, builders of sleek kayaks, masters of swift dog teams, whale hunters, listeners at the breathing places in the ice.

Because his father had always been a clever hunter, Tiktaliktak had grown up knowing only good times in the house of his family. There had always been great sea beasts for feasting, fat red trout, snow geese, and sometimes meat from the swift herds of caribou that roved beyond the mountains on the inland plain.

There had also been singing and laughter in the house of his father, and hunters from distant camps had come to visit, bringing with them their whole families.

But at the end of this winter, the animals had fled from the plain. The birds had not yet returned from the south, and the fish remained locked beneath the frozen lakes.

The wind had blown in the wrong direction during the moons of February and March, holding masses of loose ice against the shores so that no man could travel or hunt on the sea. It was a time for starving.

Tiktaliktak thought of his family lying in the dark snowhouse without food for themselves or seal oil for their lamps. Hunger stirred within him. He knew he must find a way to help them.

The young Eskimo climbed carefully down from his high place on the ice through the great pieces that surrounded him like sharp white teeth. The sea ice that lay before him had been broken many times. It had opened and closed and frozen again until he did not know where to place his feet for fear of falling through. In some places, the ice was much thicker than the height of a man; in other spots, it was thinner than his little finger. A light layer of new snow covered everything, hiding the danger from his eyes.

Before each step, Tiktaliktak felt the ice in front of him with the chisel on the end of his harpoon. Many times the sharp point broke through the thin surface and water flooded over the snow at his feet. He was forced to try one way and then another before finding ice strong enough to hold his weight. He moved forward cautiously, so that it took a long time to travel even a short distance.

Tiktaliktak was lean and strong for his age, with a handsome tanned face, wide cheekbones, and a fine hawklike nose. Like all the people of his race, he possessed quick dark eyes with the lids drawn narrow for protection against long winters on the treeless plain, where they hunted in the wind and sun and snow. He wore narrow-slitted sun goggles.

His square white teeth flashed when he smiled, and his jaw muscles, strong from eating meat, showed clearly. His hair hung straight and black almost to his shoulders. It glistened in the cold morning sunlight like the bright new wings of an Arctic butterfly, and the butterfly was Tiktaliktak's namesake.

Tiktaliktak wished most of all to be a good hunter. He could already throw a harpoon with great skill and drive an arrow straight to its mark. He thrilled at the songs and chant-

11

ing and the great whirling and drumming of the hunters as they performed the autumn and midwinter dances before the hunt.

But the magic of the dancers, and all their hunts, had failed them this year.

As he moved slowly forward testing the ice, Tiktaliktak saw before him the trail made by a huge white bear. Each of its paws had left a mark in the snow as large as if a man had sat down. Looking closely, Tiktaliktak could see that the tracks were fresh and new, for the print of each pad was still sharp and clear.

The bear must have been hungry, too, for its track led away from the land, which meant it had been forced to make the long crossing in search of new hunting grounds. Tiktaliktak hoped that the bear had not seen him, for he did not wish to fight on this thin ice. Farther along, he could see where the bear's immense weight had broken through the ice, but this meant nothing to the huge beast with its thick waterproof fur. It had crawled out of the freezing water and continued on its way.

Tiktaliktak traveled until late afternoon. Ahead of him lay the dark stretch of sea water beyond the ice. Half hidden in the winter fog above the water flew thousands of seabirds in thick black flocks. They gave the young hunter new strength,

for he knew that there must also be seals in the dark water,
and the birds and seals would provide food and oil for the
lamps of his people.

Small icebergs caught and frozen fast towered above his
head, offering him shelter in their weird shadowy blue caves.
In the haze beyond them, water and ice and sky seemed to
blend into one. The pale orange sun was surrounded by a
great circle of light. In this circle appeared four false suns and
beyond them four more. These reflections, called sun dogs,
were seldom seen, and Tiktaliktak knew they were a warning
of storms to come. His people believed them to be the team of
dogs pulling the sun on its endless journey through the sky.

When Tiktaliktak reached the edge of the sea ice, he saw

14

many flocks of birds upon the water. Excitedly, he began to plan the hunt. He would hide downwind of the birds, behind a large piece of upturned ice near the water's edge. The rafts of birds would drift near enough for his arrows to reach them, and when hit, the birds would float in to him.

Nearer and nearer drifted the birds, in countless screaming numbers. Tiktaliktak's arrows flew straight, and the birds they hit floated in as he had hoped, all save one small seabird that floated past the point where he was hiding and was blown by the wind to the far edge of the ice.

When his last arrow was gone, Tiktaliktak stood up. A few birds took off in panic, and then the others followed in great flights. They flew down the coast beyond his sight.

Tiktaliktak picked the soft warm feathered birds out of the water, and after recovering his arrows, he piled them on the ice and started out after the small bird that had drifted beyond him. With much difficulty, he finally reached it with his harpoon and pulled it to the edge of the ice. When he turned to retrace his steps to the pile of birds, a huge crack had opened in the ice, barring his path. It was too wide to jump. Tiktaliktak realized with horror that he could not return. He was drifting out to sea on a large pan of ice, carried by the rising wind and tide.

It was growing colder and soon would be dark. Tiktaliktak squatted on the ice and ate the small seabird, thinking of the precious pile of food only a short distance away. He would never see it again, nor perhaps his home.

He felt somewhat better after eating the bird and with his short knife tried to pry loose some ice to build a small snowhouse. But all he could manage was to stand some flat pieces upright, leaning them together like a tent. The cracks between the ice he filled with snow to complete a rough protection against the night wind. Curled up in this tiny shelter, he dared not sleep for fear of freezing.

All through the night, the small ice island moved with the tide. It sighed and groaned, and he wondered if it would break apart and cast him into the freezing sea.

When dawn came, he walked around his tiny frozen island,

waving his arms to warm himself. He wondered about his family and what they must be thinking.

The open water around his moving ice floe sent moisture into the freezing air. It rose as a dark fog against the pale light of morning and fell back into the leaden sea, covering his ice floe with countless frost crystals that turned it into a silent, shimmering magic place.

Suddenly, a seal's dark head came up through the water close to the edge of the ice. Tiktaliktak was ready with his harpoon, but the seal was frightened at finding itself so near a human and quickly ducked beneath the surface before the sharp point could reach him. To bring the seal back, Tiktaliktak began to call the words, "Kilee, kilee, kilee," (Come, come, come). Then he lay on the edge of the ice floe and, with the end of his knife, reached over and gently scratched just below the surface of the freezing water, imitating the sound of a seal's front claws opening a breathing hole in the ice. This sound often makes a curious seal come near. But not this one, nor did any other appear, though Tiktaliktak continued with magic words and scratching until well past midday.

In the afternoon, he walked around his small floating ice island, trying to keep warm, until a new cold wind came out of the northeast, chilling his very bones and changing the direction of his drifting home.

He improved his icehouse as much as he could and spread fresh snow on the floor to serve as a bed, for he would be warmer lying on snow than on ice. Before he lay down, he put one of his sealskin mits beneath his hip and the other beneath his shoulder.

That night, Tiktaliktak drew his arms inside his fur parka, hugging them close to his body so they would not freeze, and he breathed into his hood to help warm himself. In this way, he managed to sleep, dreaming all night of eating rich haunches of caribou, fat young loons, and the sweet summer eggs of snow geese.

As the first light of dawn crept around his tiny house, Tiktaliktak felt a gentle bump and then another. Rising quickly, he went outside the ice shelter.

His island had drifted against another much larger ice pan. Gathering his precious harpoon, bow and arrows, and his short knife, he ran lightly to the edge of the ice. First he tested the strength of the larger pan with the end of his harpoon; then he leaped across the narrow opening just as the two pieces began to draw apart.

This second drifting island felt much stronger as he walked carefully over it, feeling beneath the snow covering with his ice chisel. It did not have as many cracks or thin dangerous places as the first pan.

Through the narrow slits of his snow goggles, Tiktaliktak saw something dark spread out on the snow before him. As he hurried toward it, a huge black raven rose up and flew away. The dark stain was a patch of blood on the snow where, as the tracks leading up to it showed, a white bear had killed a seal. But, alas, the bear and almost all the seal meat were gone. Only one small fatty scrap remained, for the hungry raven had carefully cleaned away everything else left by the bear.

Nearby, Tiktaliktak found some large flat pieces of ice and started to build a new shelter. He soon tired because he was so hungry, but he continued to work until his house was completed. Then he placed the scrap of meat beside a small hole in the roof and crawled inside to wait.

Before long, he heard the swish of wings as the raven returned. The sleek black bird landed on the spot where the
seal had been and, finding nothing, rose up with an angry
croak. It landed again, this time on top of Tiktaliktak's house,
ready to snatch the last remaining morsel of seal fat.

In an instant, Tiktaliktak's hand shot up through the hole,
grasped the raven's leg, and pulled it down into the house.
Some say ravens are not good to eat; they are wrong. The
raven was thin but delicious, and Tiktaliktak felt much better
after this fine breakfast.

For three days and three nights, he walked about on his floe to warm himself and slept when he could. The winds and strong tides moved his island back and forth, sometimes out to sea, sometimes toward the land. He found nothing more to eat and felt he would surely die on this lonely ice island.

On the fourth day, Tiktaliktak awoke and sensed that something had changed. He looked out of his house, and there before him was the most welcome sight he had ever seen. In the distance, like a gigantic stony cloud, lay the island called Sakkiak, its raw granite hills piercing through the surrounding shore ice. These hills were swept entirely free of snow by the wind. Tiktaliktak knew that no man dared to live on Sakkiak, but it was solid rock, and he longed to leave his ice island and place his foot upon it, though it was a bleak and lonely place.

He judged the drift of his ice pan with great care and saw that he would come close to the shore ice surrounding the large island. He realized, too, that his ice floe might not touch it and might be swept forever out into the open sea.

Tiktaliktak planned now to try a desperate trick he had once heard of. If it failed, he would surely die.

He ran to the thinnest corner of his floating island where he had noticed a piece of ice that had cracked off and then partly refrozen. It was not much larger than a walrus, but if he could break it loose, it might keep him afloat and serve as a clumsy boat. He worked frantically with his chisel, trying to

free the corner as he drew nearer and nearer to the long floe of loose ice stretching out from the island. He could see now that he would pass the long floe without touching.

Suddenly, the small piece of ice broke beneath his chisel and was free. With a quick jump, he landed upon it and, kneeling down, paddled desperately with his hands in the freezing water. The ice boat was moving, and in a short time he touched against the loose ice that stretched in a wide broken path to the island.

Now came the most daring part of the trick. Arranging his bow and arrow quiver so they hung straight down his back and holding his harpoon with both hands before him at the

23

level of his chest to steady his balance, Tiktaliktak started running and jumping from pan to pan with every bit of skill he possessed.

If he dared to stop even for a moment, the small pieces of ice would roll or sink in the icy water and he would fall. He moved with the balance and delicacy of a sandpiper skirting a wave on a beach until he made a final leap onto the strong shore ice surrounding the island. There he lay, gasping.

As his breath returned to him, Tiktaliktak could scarcely believe that he had reached solid ice and was still alive. Slowly he walked toward the sheltering hills of the great barren island that rose before him, grateful to be on land once more.

He chose a valley that formed a long sheltered passage leading upward to the top of the island. In this valley, under the protecting hills, he built a small strong snowhouse and slept he knew not how long. After this, he lost all track of time.

Tiktaliktak awoke with raging pangs of hunger and hurried out to see what treasures his new island might provide. Weak as he was from lack of food, it took a full day to walk the length of the island. Although Sakkiak was fairly narrow, it also took him a day to cross it because of the steep rocky spine of hills that ran its whole length.

The beaches were blown almost clear. Snow had been driven against the hills in hard wind-packed drifts many times the height of a man. Tiktaliktak walked along the frozen beaches,

25

searching them for any kind of food and peering out hopefully over the shore ice for seals.

Nothing did he see but snow and rock and sometimes bleached white bones or hard dry scraps of bird skins eaten out a season before by foxes. The lemmings, small rodents without tails, seemed not to be on the island, for he saw no tracks. The fat eider ducks had left evidence everywhere, in the form of old nesting places, of their summer occupation of the island. But by the time they returned to lay their eggs, he would surely be dead of hunger.

Often he gazed out across the straits, where the white ice floes churned past in the dangerous rip tides. He could see the mainland hanging blue and serene like a dream of some far-off place. There was his home, his family, his friends. All of them must think that he was dead. The mainland seemed near, and yet to Tiktaliktak, without food or materials or a boat, it was an impossible distance.

Staggering from hunger and fatigue, he returned to the snowhouse that evening and had terrible dreams until he awoke in the morning in the cold gray igloo scarcely knowing whether he was truly awake or still in some dark nightmare.

When he climbed the hill the next day, Tiktaliktak used his harpoon for support, like an old man. He had to tell himself again and again that he had lived fewer than twenty summers.

From the top of the rocky hill, Tiktaliktak saw far out on the drifting ice many walrus, fat, sleek, and brown, lying together motionless like great stones, their tusks showing white in the sunlight. The wind was carrying them away, out to sea, and he could never hope to take one.

Sitting there in the cold wind, with no help, he said aloud, over and over again, "This island is my grave. This island is my grave. I shall never leave this place. I shall never leave this place." The idea obsessed him, and at last, in fright, he hurriedly stumbled downward, falling many times, until he came to the snowhouse and slept again for a very long while.

When he awoke, Tiktaliktak cut small strips from the tops of his boots and chewed them to ease his hunger. This seemed to give him some strength. Then, slowly, as if drawn by magic, he started again up the long hill.

It was warmer now. True spring was coming to the land. But it helped him not at all, for there was nothing living on the island, nor would there be until the birds came to nest again, and that would be too late for him.

On top of the hill once more, Tiktaliktak scanned the sea and saw nothing but water and glaring ice. Again a distant voice seemed to say, "This island is your grave." He stood up slowly and looked around. There were many great flat rocks, and Tiktaliktak decided they would be his final resting place. Two of the largest ones lay near each other, offering him a sheltered bed, and with his failing strength, he dragged two more large stones to make the ends, at head and foot. Another large one placed on top covered the lower half. The stones now formed a rough coffin.

He searched until he found a large flat piece to cover his head. Half laughing and half crying, he climbed into his stony grave. After one last look at the wide blue sky and the sea around him, he lay down with his harpoon, knife, and bow arranged neatly by his side. He hoped that his relatives would someday find his bones and know him by his weapons and know what had happened to him.

Tiktaliktak did not know how long he slept. When he awoke, he was numb with cold. Slowly, a new idea started to form in

his mind. "I will not die, I will not die, I will not die." With a great effort, he pushed away the stone that formed the top half of the coffin. Painfully, he arose and staggered out of that self-made grave.

Holding himself as straight as he could with the aid of his harpoon, Tiktaliktak staggered down the side of the hill to the beach. He lay there to rest and again fell asleep. This time he dreamed of many strange things: skin boats rising up from their moorings, haunches of fat year-old caribou, rich dark walrus meat, young ducks with delicious yellow fat, juicy seals, and the warm eggs of a snow owl.

He could not tell if he was asleep or awake, but again and again the head of a seal appeared. It seemed so real in the dream that he took up his harpoon and cast it blindly before

him. He felt a great jerk that fully awakened him, and, behold, he had a true seal firmly harpooned. He lay back with his feet against a rock and held onto the harpoon line until the seal's spirit left him.

With his last strength, Tiktaliktak drew the seal out of the water and across the edge of the ice until he had all this richness in his hands. He knew that the seal had been sent to him by the sea spirit and that this gift would give him back his life.

After some food and sleep, and more food and sleep again, he soon felt well. Using his bow, he whirled an arrow swiftly into a hollow scrap of driftwood and dried shavings until they grew hot, smoked, and burst into flames. The seal fat burned nicely in a hollow stone in his snowhouse, making it warm and bright. The spring sun helped to restore his health and strength, and Tiktaliktak remembered once more that he was young.

He kept the meat of the seal in the igloo and prepared the fat for use in the stone lamp. The sealskin he turned inside out without splitting it open and scraped it with a flattened bone in the special way that he had seen his mother teach his sister.

One day, he found the tracks of a white fox that had come to the island. After that, the fox came to visit his dwelling every day. It always came along the same way, and that was its mistake. Tiktaliktak built a falling-stone trap across its path, baited with a scrap of seal meat.

The next morning, the fox was in the trap, and after skinning it, Tiktaliktak drew from the tail long strong sinews that make the finest thread. That evening he ate the fox meat and placed the fine white skin above his oil lamp to dry. Tiktaliktak also made a good needle by sharpening a thin splinter of bone on a rock, and with this, he mended his clothes.

After his work was done, he stepped out through the entrance of the small igloo to look at the great night sky. It was filled with stars beyond counting that formed patterns familiar to all his people, who used them for guidance when traveling.

Off to the north, great green and yellow lights soared up, slowly faded, then soared again in their magic way. Tiktaliktak's people knew that these were caused by the night spirits playing the kicking game in the sky. In the way his father had taught him, he whistled and pushed his hands up to the sky, marveling as the lights ebbed and flowed with his movements as though he controlled them.

Life on the island was better now, but still Tiktaliktak longed to return home to his own people.

Half of another moon passed, and now the spring sun hung just below the horizon each night and would not let the sky grow dark. Two seals appeared in the open waters of the bay in front of the snowhouse, and by good fortune, Tiktaliktak managed to harpoon first one and then the other. This gave him an abundance of food and of oil to heat his igloo. He again carefully drew the meat out of the seals, without cutting them open in the usual method, and scraped and dried the skins.

Tiktaliktak sat before his small house thinking and making plans. An idea for building a kind of boat without any tools or driftwood for the frame had finally come to him.

He began to prepare one of the three sealskins. First, he tied the skin tightly and carefully where the back flippers had been so that no water could enter. Then where the seal's neck had been, he bound in a piece of bone, hollow through the middle. When he had finished, he put his mouth to the hole and, with many strong breaths, blew the skin up so that it looked again like a fat seal. Next, he fitted a small piece of driftwood in the bone to act as a plug and hold in the air.

The sun was warm on his back as he worked with his floats on that bright spring morning. His stomach was full, his clothes were mended, and he began to make a song inside himself, hoping that someday he might return to his people on the mainland. The song had magic in it. It spoke of fear and wonder and of life and hope. The words came well. There was joy in Tiktaliktak and yet a warning of danger, too.

He looked up from his work as a huge shadow loomed over him. Tiktaliktak threw himself sideways, rolling toward his harpoon, which he caught hold of as he sprang to his feet. Before him, between his small house and the sea, stood a huge white bear. The bear's mouth was half open, and its blue-black tongue lolled between its strong teeth. Its little eyes were watching him warily as it decided how best to kill him.

Fear stirred the hair on the back of Tiktaliktak's neck and reached down into his stomach. His harpoon was small for a beast such as this one, and although he had often heard of encounters with bears, Tiktaliktak had never met one face to face.

Remembering the wise words of his father, Tiktaliktak carefully studied every movement of the bear. He tried to think like a bear to understand what the great beast would do next.

He slowly knelt down and felt with the chisel end of the harpoon for a crack between two rocks. Finding this, he wedged it in firmly and leveled the pointed end at the bear's throat. He had not long to wait for the attack.

The bear lunged forward, and the harpoon pierced the white fur and went deep into its throat. Tiktaliktak held the harpoon as long as he could, then rolled away, but not before he felt the bear's great claws rake the side of his face. He scrambled to his feet and ran uphill.

The huge beast tried to follow, but the harpoon caught and caught again in the rocks, forcing the point more deeply inward. The harpoon found its life, and with a great sigh, the bear's spirit rushed out and it was dead.

Tiktaliktak's face was numb at first. Then it started to throb with pain. He made his way slowly to a small hillside stream that flowed from the melting snow down to the sea. There he washed his face in the clear icy water.

Returning to his snowhouse, he took a patch of foxskin the size of his hand, scraped and scrubbed it clean, and set it squarely over the terrible wound. As it dried, the clean patch of foxskin tightened and grew smaller. It drew the open wounds together almost forming a new skin on his face.

Tiktaliktak was weak after his fight with the bear and nervous of every shadow. Also, he feared that his wound might fester, so he washed the foxskin dressing often. In time, his face showed signs of healing, and the pain ceased to bother him.

Then Tiktaliktak set about making a little stone and sod house for the summer like the ancient houses of his forefathers. He had no material to make the kind of sealskin tent now used by his people.

Inside the new house, it was warm and comfortable, and the light from his small lamp glowed brightly. The new bearskin was warm to sleep on and the meat good to eat. At this time, another seal came to him one evening in the half dark of spring before the moon had fully risen. It did not see Tiktaliktak until his harpoon reached it.

Cutting this seal open in the usual way, from the rear flippers to the throat, Tiktaliktak then scraped and stretched the skin. With the skin, he made new hip-length boot tops to sew above his own. These bound with drawstrings and packed with dried moss were quite waterproof.

He had placed the two shoulder blades of the white bear under a stone in the water so that the sea lice would pick them clean as snow. He now bound them firmly with seal thongs to each end of his harpoon. In this way, he made a strong double-bladed paddle.

On a windless day, he tied the three blown-up sealskins together and placed them in the shallow water. Sitting astride them, he balanced himself and floated. It took some practice before he was able to hold steady and paddle and control this strange craft, but a boat of any kind seemed his only chance of reaching the mainland again.

By day, Tiktaliktak would look out over the great expanse of water with its treacherous tides and wonder if he had lived through this terrible spring only to drown. At night, he would dream of his mother, his father, and his sisters. He wondered if they had starved or had found food as he had and were still alive.

He must try to make the crossing. First, he gathered a small parcel of meat, which he wrapped in seal fat so it would float and covered with sealskin so that it would be protected from the salt of the sea. Tiktaliktak tied the package to his waist with a thong, and it floated nicely behind him like a small duck. He filled two seal bladder pouches with fresh water, and these he hung around his neck.

The next morning was gray with fog, but the wind was down, and he decided this would be the day to start the dangerous journey. Pushing the inflated sealskin floats into the water, Tiktaliktak carefully climbed onto the strange water-craft. Then he started out, with only one glance back at his island home and upward to his open grave on top of the hill.

Cautiously, he began to use the bone paddle to steer out into the current, which swirled away from the island and carried him into the open water of the strait. With alarm, he noticed the great strength of the tide as it swept him eastward instead of north to the mainland as he had hoped. Tiktaliktak paddled very gently, careful not to upset his frail craft, learning as he went to guide it with his feet, which hung down awkwardly like those of a young snow goose trying to swim for the first time.

Tiktaliktak tried not to look down, for he could see far below him in the clear gray water great fronds of seaweed waving mysteriously, moved by powerful underwater currents. A light breeze rippled over the surface of the water, sending him out toward the center of the strait. He could see the rip-tides now pressing down or swelling upward in a smooth icy rush. His feet and legs began to feel the freezing grip of the water, although they stayed dry. The chill of the sea drove through his boots, moss packing, and heavy fur socks, leaving him numb with cold.

Slowly, the hills of Sakkiak grew smaller and turned blue in the distance. Tiktaliktak judged himself to be halfway to the mainland. He paddled gently to give himself direction in the fast-moving current and was carried on the tide through gray patches of mist that hung over the water. Now stiff with cold and thirsty, he managed to drink a little of the fresh water from one of the pouches that hung around his neck and pad-dled on through the eerie silence.

Suddenly, Tiktaliktak heard a familiar sound, a sound he feared. It boomed across the water again and again, the great grunting roar of a huge bull walrus. The tide was carrying him straight into the herd the walrus was jealously protecting.

Dark heads appeared as the large herd grouped together, peering weak-eyed at this new intruder. Almost all of them showed the long thin tusks of female walrus.

The old bull separated from the herd, ready for combat. It started to rear up in the water, trying to see and also to frighten the new enemy, while working itself into a fury. Tiktaliktak knew that to the poor eyesight of the beast he would look like another walrus trying to enter the herd.

With a roaring bellow, the great bull, flashing its white tusks, dove beneath the surface and went straight at Tiktaliktak. He braced himself, expecting to be lifted from the water, when to his surprise the old bull rose up before him locked in combat with a powerful young male walrus.

Tiktaliktak watched them struggle, their tusks ripping and

locking, their eyes rolling. The water around them frothed white and then turned red with blood.

By good fortune, helped by the tide and steady paddling, Tiktaliktak was carried safely away. The huge struggling beasts thrashed in the sea, never noticing that he had drifted onward.

Seabirds screamed around him, and he felt the welcome pull of the tide as it drew him at last toward the shores of the

mainland. The dark granite cliffs seemed to tower over him when he drifted into their shadows. Delicate lacings of snow on the cliffs glowed in the long rays of the evening sun.

Suddenly, with a bump that almost upset him, Tiktaliktak felt solid rock beneath his feet. He stumbled ashore, scarcely able to stand on his numb, nearly frozen legs. Looking back over the waters he had crossed, he was filled with gratitude that the spirits who guard the land and sea and sky had allowed him to make his dangerous journey.

Dragging behind him the three inflated sealskins, Tiktaliktak struggled over the rocky beach while the first shower of summer rain beat against his face. With his knife, he cut the thongs that held the bone paddle blades to his harpoon, and it again became his weapon. He then cut the three skin floats open from end to end, and placing the dry inside of one beneath himself, he stretched the other two over himself and fell deeply asleep.

He was awakened by the damp cold the next morning. The mists of early summer hung down everywhere, obscuring the cliffs and the seabirds that cried above him.

Joyful at the thought of being once again on the mainland after so many moons, he jumped up, ate some of the meat in his small package, drank some fresh water from a nearby stream, and set out along the coast toward the west. Although Tiktaliktak had never traveled in this part of the country before, he knew it would be easier and safer to stay on the coast than to risk a straighter path across the mountains. Climbing would use up his strength, and perhaps he would lose his way.

Tiktaliktak walked for two long days and slept at night under rock ledges like a wild animal. Then he came to a narrow inlet that he had never seen before, but he recognized it from his grandfather's description as the bay called "The Place of Beautiful Stones."

Walking fearfully along the edge of the small half-hidden cove, it did indeed seem like a place from another world. The gray rock cliffs that stood above him had the weird forms of ancient giants. At the end of the small bay, a well-worn path led up to the mouth of a dark cave in the crumbling rock wall.

Tiktaliktak stood before it in the gloom of the late afternoon listening for some sound, almost afraid to enter, yet eager to see for himself the inside of this strange place.

Hearing nothing save the dripping of water, he bent down and stepped quickly into the cave. Its entrance was small, but the cave was large inside and rose to a great height. When his eyes grew accustomed to the half darkness, he knelt down and examined the floor of the cave.

It was covered with smooth round white pebbles, and among them lay a number of shining red stones. These were so sharply cut that Tiktaliktak's people believed they could only have been shaped by strange men or spirits. There were also other

stones cut in this wondrous way, and as clear as water, they glowed like the waning moon even in the half darkness.

Tiktaliktak looked to the wall on his left, and there, just as his grandfather had said, were two neat rows of holes, exactly as many as he had fingers and toes, each containing a fox skull bleached white with age. Near these, embedded in the walls, were more red stones that seemed to wink like eyes in the fading light.

Some said that this was an ancient secret place of the little people who used to rule the land. It was here they came to collect and cut the precious stones they loved to have and to trade sometimes with other people.

Tiktaliktak gathered a few stones and would have taken more, but he heard a tapping sound deep in the cave and hurried out. He walked quickly all of that night, glad to be away from the strange place.

Throughout the next day, he slept peacefully on a moss-covered ledge above the sea. Before he fell asleep, he watched a rough-legged hawk circling high above him and heard brown female eider ducks cooing below as they plucked the soft down from their breasts to line the warm nests they were building for their young.

That evening as Tiktaliktak strode along the coast in the soft twilight of the Arctic summer, he saw the rugged coastal mountains sloping gently into the great inland plain. Crossing

the foothills, he finally reached the immense plain that stood before his homeland. Now his feet welcomed every step forward in the soft tundra.

The warm sun the next morning followed its course through the eastern sky, and small bright flowers burst into bloom everywhere. The edge of each pond was made beautiful by patches of white Arctic cotton that swayed in the light breeze. Best of all, his namesake, the butterfly, traveled in a straight line before him and seemed to guide him on the long journey homeward.

Now he saw many caribou lying on the hillside with their brown backs blending into the land itself, their antlers covered in thick summer velvet. Tiktaliktak ran for joy to think that he was once again in a place of plenty.

He waded straight across wide shallow lakes, whose water came no higher than his knees, and through streams where every step sent fat sea trout darting away like silver arrows. As he traveled, he crossed high sandy beaches covered with shells, where the sea had washed in ancient times.

At last, he looked across the valley and recognized the three familiar hills that stood before his home—Telik, Egalalik, and Ashivak. Soon he would be among his own people. Were they alive? He was almost afraid to know.

He hurried down the gravel slope, across the boulder-strewn floor of the valley that had once been the bed of an immense river, up through the mossy pass between Egalalik and Ashivak, and up the rise past the small lake where his family took their water for drinking. There lay his sister's sealskin water bucket beside a freshly worn path. They must be living still.

Tiktaliktak sat down beside the path and thought. "If I appear before them quickly, they will think I am a ghost or spirit, for they must surely believe I am dead."

Getting up, he peered around a large rock down into that beloved valley. There was the big sealskin tent of his family, and beyond it the tent of his uncle, and a little farther up the valley, the family tents of Tauki and Kungo. Tiktaliktak saw his mother bending over at the entrance to their tent with her head deep in her hood, as was the custom of his people when sad. He saw his sister Sharni carrying something that looked like clothing. She took this to her mother, who placed it on a small pile before her. A moment later, Tiktaliktak saw his father step out of their tent and gaze toward the sea.

In the long shadows of early morning, he saw Kungo and his family, soon followed by the others, walk down toward his father's tent. Although it was not cold, they all had their hoods drawn over their heads in sadness and wore their oldest clothes. Tiktaliktak wondered how he could let them know he had returned without frightening them.

He walked back until he reached the edge of the hill behind the camp, where he knew his figure would be seen easily against the morning sky. Now he moved slowly. Kungo's sharp eyes saw him first. Tiktaliktak watched him point and call to the others in a low hunter's voice. In a moment, they were all looking at him on the skyline.

"Who is that?" said Kungo's daughter.

"Can it be?" asked his sister.

"That person has the shape of Tiktaliktak and his way of walking," said Tauki.

Tiktaliktak coughed twice, and they all said, "That is his cough. He coughs in that way."

Then someone said, "Ghost," and another said, "Spirit," and he could see they were all about to run away.

"Relatives," he called in a soft, ordinary voice. "I have returned. I am glad to see you all again." And he sat down on a rock and started to chant and sing a funny little song his mother had taught them as children.

Sharni, his sister, called, "Brother of mine, that must be the real you singing that song and no ghost!"

Tiktaliktak answered, "Sister of mine, it is really me. May I come down to you and visit?"

They all began to talk at once. Then Tiktaliktak's father called to him, "Come forward," and he walked out bravely, alone, to meet this ghost, or perhaps his returning son, halfway between the hill and camp.

Tiktaliktak's father looked frightened and suspicious. But coming up to his son, he reached out timidly, touched his arm, and tenderly ran his hand over the great new scars on his son's face. He then passed his hand across his eyes, and feeling tears in them, he leaned forward and gave Tiktaliktak a hug that nearly broke his bones.

In a voice ringing with joy, his father called to his wife and daughters and all the others, saying that this was no ghost but a real person and that, on the very day that they were to give his clothes away, their son at long last had returned home to them.

Tiktaliktak's mother and sisters led him gently into the dark skin tent and seated him on their wide bed made of sweet-smelling summer heather covered with soft, thick winter caribou skins.

They drew off the long worn-out sealskin boots that he had made and replaced them with warm fur slippers. Slowly, they fed him many of the good things he had dreamed of during his long adventure.

When Tiktaliktak could eat no more, he lay back on the rich warm skins, feeling full of food and contentment. His family was well, and he was overjoyed to be alive and once again in the tent of his father. He closed his eyes and drifted peacefully toward sleep.

In his mind's eye, there arose a shining vision of his island home. Sakkiak now seemed to him a warm and friendly place, for it had become a part of his life, a part of himself.

Tiktaliktak's song floated down to him from the sky. Each word had found its proper place. He could feel himself swaying to the rhythm of the big drum that beat inside him, and he heard the long answering chorus of women's voices in some distant dance house. His mind, knowing the words, started singing softly:

Ayii, yaii,
Ayii, yaii,
The great sea
Has set me in motion,
Set me adrift,
And I moved
As a weed moves
In the river.

The arch of sky
And mightiness of storms
Encompassed me,
And I am left
Trembling with joy,
Ayii, yaii,
Ayii, yaii.